Boswell Wide Awake

ALEXANDRA DAY

Farrar Straus Giroux
New York

Distributed in Canada by Douglas & McIntyre Ltd.

Library of Congress catalog card number: 98-75733

Color separations by Prestige Graphics

Printed and bound in the United States of America by Berryville Graphics

Typography by Filomena Tuosto

First edition, 1999

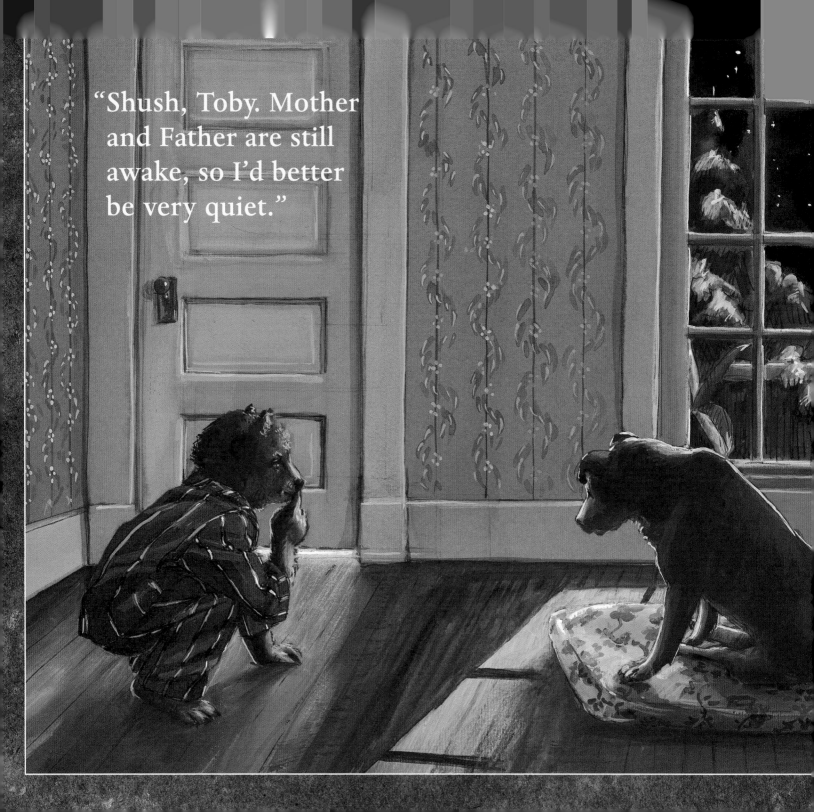

"Shush, Toby. Mother and Father are still awake, so I'd better be very quiet."

"There! Now you can go to sleep, Fish."

"Look, Cat, someone left the kitchen light on."

"Here, kitty, kitty. What are you doing out there, Cat?"

"Have a good sleep, Cat."

"Good night, Father."

"Good night, Mother."